E
N I   Nims, Bonnie Larkin

Where is the bear?

$9.95

DATE			
JY 06 '88	MR 21 '90	AG 7 '91	MAY 4 '94
	AP 20 '90	SE 26 '91	JUN 30 '94
JY 22 '88	MY 5 '90		JUL 21 '94
OC 14 '88	MY 29 '90	JY 9 '92	AUG 1 '94
DE 13 '88	JY 3 '90	JY 23 '92	AUG 17 '94
JY 11 '89	JY 23 '90	SE 4 '93	FEB 08 '95
JY 31 '89	AG 2 '90	SE 29 '93	MAR 09 '95
AG 31 '89	SE 19 '90	OC 13 '93	MAY 3 1 '95
OC 3 '89	OC 11 '90	OC 28 '93	JUN 20 '95
	AP 18 '91		JUL 05 '95
OC 20 '89	JY 11 '91	NOV 30 '93	OCT 09 '95
DE 18 '89	JY 26 '91	DEC 23 '93	AUG 01 '96
			SEP 23 '96
			AUG 14 '96

© THE BAKER & TAYLOR CO.

Where Is the Bear?

Bonnie Larkin Nims
pictures by
John and Alex Wallner

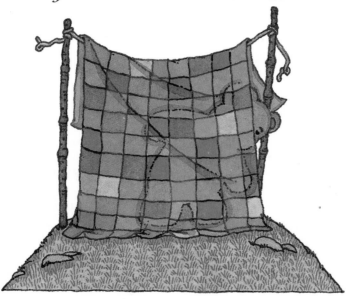

Albert Whitman & Company

Niles, Illinois

Library of Congress Cataloging in Publication Data

Nims, Bonnie Larkin.

　Where is the bear?

　Summary: Rhyming text asks the reader to find the
hidden bear in each scene, with varying degrees
of difficulty.
　[1. Bears—Fiction. 2. Literary recreations.
3. Stories in rhyme] I. Wallner, John C., ill.
II. Wallner, Alexandra. III. Title.
PZ8.3.N6Wh 1988　　　　[E]　　　　87-25321
ISBN 0-8075-8933-0

Because of James, Jeremy, and Elliot . . . *B.N.*
For Fanny, a little bear lost. *J.W. & A.W.*

See the bear?
You'll find him hiding,
if you look
at every picture
in this book . . .

I see a baby girl
laughing in her chair
as her cup and her bowl
twirl through the air.

But I am looking for a bear.
Can you show me—
where is the bear?

I see a merry-go-round
and there's a very tall slide,
where up is a long, long climb
and down is an easy ride.

But I am looking for a bear.
Can you show me—
where is the bear?

I see buses and cars
rushing to, rushing fro,
and the light that tells
when to stop, when to go.

But I am looking for a bear.
Can you show me—
where is the bear?

I see carts filled with boxes and cans,
with fruits and vegetables, too,
and every now and then,
there's a baby peeking through.

But I am looking for a bear.
Can you show me—
where is the bear?

I see a barn bursting with hay—
hay in the window, hay on the floor—
and one-two-three horses
trotting out the door.

But I am looking for a bear.
Can you show me—
where is the bear?

I see a brand-new rainbow
shimmering across the sky.
I see a brand-new puddle
shining as bright as your eye.

But I am looking for a bear.
Can you show me—
where is the bear?

I see a juggler juggling,
and there's a clowning clown,
and a band that's nice and noisy
marching through the town.

But I am looking for a bear.
Can you show me—
where is the bear?

I see lions taking a snooze,
monkeys with ear-to-ear grins,
and a big family of elephants
not big enough for their skins!

But I am looking for a bear.
Can you show me—
where is the bear?

I see the moon keeping watch
and a little boy asleep in his bed—
or maybe that's a little girl
with the covers pulled over her head.

But I am looking for a bear.
Can you show me—
where is the bear?

Bonnie Nims has worked as an advertising copywriter, an editor-in-chief of an eighteen-volume children's encyclopedia, and a producer/writer/editor of audio-visual materials, but her chief love has always been writing for children. "From the time I first learned to read," she says, "I wanted to write children's books. I found so much pleasure in reading them that I felt writing for children would be the most valuable and satisfying work I could ever hope to do."

Bonnie is the author of two previous books for young people and of numerous stories and poems. Her work has appeared widely in readers and language-arts textbooks.

She lives on the shore of Lake Michigan in Chicago with her husband, the poet John Frederick Nims. They have three children and three grandchildren.

John and *Alexandra Wallner* live in a 150-year-old remodeled farmhouse in Woodstock, New York, with their West Highland white terrier, Mona, and four cats, Willoughby, Renfield, Buster, and Ollie. In the spring and summer months, they enjoy working in their garden; in the winter, they enjoy stoking and sitting by their wood stoves.

John has illustrated over fifty books, and Alex has written and illustrated several books and numerous textbooks for young children. *Where Is the Bear?* is the second book they have worked on together.